Bess marched over to where George was standing.

"Georgia Fayne, don't you dare ignore me!" Bess said. "Nancy is trying to find my locket—the one *you* lost! How can you stand there reading that stupid newspaper?"

"Oh, sure," George said. "My soccer game is stupid. But your stupid locket is the most important thing in the whole world!"

When George said that, Bess's face turned bright red. She grabbed the newspaper clipping.

"I hope your team loses every game for the rest of the year!" Bess yelled. Then she tore the newspaper into a dozen tiny pieces—and threw them on the ground!

The Nancy Drew Notebooks

#1 The Slumber Party Secret
#2 The Lost Locket

Available from MINSTREL Books

For orders other than by individual consumers, Minstrel Books grants a discount on the purchase of **10 or more** copies of single titles for special markets or premium use. For further details, please write to the Vice-President of Special Markets, Pocket Books, 1230 Avenue of the Americas, New York, NY 10020.

For information on how individual consumers can place orders, please write to Mail Order Department, Paramount Publishing, 200 Old Tappan Road, Old Tappan, NJ 07675.

THE NANCY DREW NOTEBOOKS™

#2

THE LOST LOCKET

CAROLYN KEENE

Illustrated by Anthony Accardo

A MINSTREL® BOOK

PUBLISHED BY POCKET BOOKS

New York   London   Toronto   Sydney   Tokyo   Singapore

The sale of this book without its cover is unauthorized. If you purchased this book without a cover, you should be aware that it was reported to the publisher as "unsold and destroyed." Neither the author nor the publisher has received payment for the sale of this "stripped book."

This book is a work of fiction. Names, characters, places, and incidents are products of the author's imagination or are used fictitiously. Any resemblance to actual events or locales or persons, living or dead, is entirely coincidental.

A MINSTREL PAPERBACK *ORIGINAL*

 A Minstrel Book published by
POCKET BOOKS, a division of Simon & Schuster Inc.
1230 Avenue of the Americas, New York, NY 10020

Copyright © 1994 by Simon & Schuster Inc.
Produced by Mega-Books of New York, Inc.

All rights reserved, including the right to reproduce this book or portions thereof in any form whatsoever. For information address Pocket Books, 1230 Avenue of the Americas, New York, NY 10020

ISBN: 0-671-87946-4

First Minstrel Books printing September 1994

10 9 8 7 6 5 4 3 2 1

NANCY DREW, A MINSTREL BOOK and colophon are registered trademarks of Simon & Schuster Inc.

THE NANCY DREW NOTEBOOKS is a trademark of Simon & Schuster Inc.

Cover art by Cliff Miller

Printed in the U.S.A.

THE LOST LOCKET

1

Furious Friends

It's all your fault! I'll never forgive you. Ever!" Bess Marvin shouted at her cousin George.

Big tears filled Bess's eyes. She kicked at a pile of leaves. They had fallen from the biggest maple tree in the park.

"Don't be stupid!" George yelled back. "It's not my fault."

"It is, too!" Bess yelled.

"Is not!" George shouted. "I didn't do anything!"

"That's right!" Bess cried. "You didn't do *anything!* And now my locket is gone!"

George brushed a leaf out of her dark

1

curls. "Oh, yeah? Well, ask Nancy," George said.

She pointed to their best friend, Nancy Drew. Nancy was hurrying across the grass toward the playground. "Go on and ask her. *She'll* tell you it's not my fault."

Eight-year-old Nancy held the straps of her bright blue backpack in her right hand. She swung it back and forth as she walked through the park.

The cool October air blew through Nancy's reddish blond hair and made her feel good. It was Friday. Now she had the whole weekend to be with her friends.

"What's going on?" Nancy asked as she came up to her friends.

"George lost my locket," Bess answered. Tears streaked Bess's cheeks.

"I did not!" George said. She put her hands on her hips.

"Did, too!" Bess yelled.

"But what happened?" Nancy asked. She dropped her backpack at the base of the huge maple tree. That was where everyone always put their things when they came to the park after school.

"Tell me everything," Nancy said, looking from Bess to George. They were her two best friends. She had never seen them fight. "Is your locket really gone, Bess? The beautiful one—the fancy gold heart?"

"Yes!" Bess cried. Her voice almost cracked.

Nancy put her arm around Bess. No wonder Bess was so upset! Bess's aunt Sarah had given the locket to her for her birthday.

The locket was a gold heart that opened. Bess's name was engraved on the front. There was a tiny pearl in the middle.

"That's terrible if it's gone," Nancy said. "But will somebody just tell me what happened?"

"I'll tell you," Bess said. She pulled Nancy to one side by the arm. "Don't listen to George. She won't tell you the truth."

Bess brushed her blond hair out of

her face and adjusted her navy blue headband. When she was all set, she took a deep breath.

"I was wearing the locket," Bess said, looking only at Nancy. "And I didn't want *anything* to happen to it. But all the girls were taking turns jumping rope. I wanted to jump rope, too. So I took off my locket and handed it to George. I asked her to hold it for me while I jumped. But she didn't hold it! She put it in her backpack instead. Now it's gone."

Nancy looked at George to see what she would say. George looked unhappy.

"I didn't lose it on purpose," George explained. "I only put it in my backpack because I thought it would be safer there."

"Well, maybe it's not even gone," Nancy said. "Maybe it just fell out of your backpack into the leaves."

Nancy walked over to George's backpack near the big tree. She started to look through the leaves. But Bess stopped her.

"No. It's not in the leaves," Bess said. "I looked. It's been *stolen*. And look what the thief left instead." Bess picked up a plastic sandwich bag with a soggy sandwich inside. "This was in George's backpack."

"Yuck!" Nancy said. She could smell relish, even before she opened the bag. Relish, ketchup, and mustard were leaking all over the white bread.

"It's really gross," Bess warned her.

Nancy took the sandwich out of the bag, anyway. She held it far away from her. Then she peeled the layers of bread apart to see what was inside.

Peanut butter? With ketchup, mustard, and relish? It was all mushed together between the bread. It was the grossest sandwich Nancy had ever seen.

"Whoever stole my locket was trying to be mean," Bess said. "They left this sandwich just to make me sick!"

Nancy thought about that for a minute. It *was* a mean trick. But who would do it? And why?

Nancy looked inside George's backpack again. She checked every pocket. But the locket was not there. The only thing Nancy found was George's new notebook. The notebook was red with a silver stripe on the cover. It matched the stripe on the backpack flap.

"Don't worry," Nancy said, getting excited. "This is a mystery. And I'm good at mysteries. Maybe I can figure out who stole the locket and get it back."

"Good," Bess said. "Because if you don't, I'm never speaking to George again."

Nancy frowned. That would be terrible!

"Where exactly did George put the locket?" Nancy asked Bess. "In the big main part? Or in the little pocket?"

"Don't ask me," Bess said. "George? George! I don't believe it. Look! She's not even listening!"

Nancy looked. George had moved away. She was standing by a bench with some girls from her soccer team. She had a newspaper clipping in her hand.

7

Nancy could guess what it was—the picture of George that had been in the River Heights newspaper a few days earlier. It showed George kicking the winning goal in Monday's soccer game.

"George!" Bess yelled. "Get over here!"

George glanced over at Bess. "Just a minute," she called to her cousin. Then she went on talking to her other friends.

Bess stamped her foot and marched over to George. Nancy followed.

"Georgia Fayne, don't you dare ignore me!" Bess said, using George's full name. No one ever called her Georgia. Bess knew it would make her mad. "Nancy is trying to find my locket—the one *you* lost! How can you stand there reading that stupid newspaper?"

"*Stupid* newspaper?" George said. "Oh, sure. My soccer game is stupid. But your stupid locket is the most important thing in the whole world!"

When George said that, Bess's face turned bright red. It was exactly the color of George's backpack—except that it didn't have a silver stripe down the middle.

Bess grabbed the newspaper clipping. "I hope your team loses every game for the rest of the year!" she yelled. Then she tore the newspaper into a dozen tiny pieces—and threw them on the ground!

2
Too Many Suspects

That's it!" George said, glaring at Bess. "I don't care if you *are* my cousin. I'll never speak to you again, Bess Marvin."

"Oh, yeah? Well, that goes double for me, *Georgia* Fayne!" Bess yelled.

With that, Bess turned around and stormed out of the park.

George marched over to the tree and picked up her backpack. Then she stomped out of the park, too.

"Wait!" Nancy called. "Wait! Come back!"

But it was too late. Her friends were too far away to hear.

A lump formed in Nancy's throat. "I

10

hate it when people fight," she said out loud. "And I hate it when people walk away from me!"

Nancy wanted to run after Bess and George. But they were going in opposite directions. How could she choose?

Now her two best friends were mad at each other. Maybe they were angry at Nancy, too!

Nancy frowned. She almost wanted to cry. But she stopped herself. There was a mystery to be solved. Maybe if she found the lost locket, Bess and George would be friends again.

Nancy reached into her own backpack. She pulled out the special notebook that her father had given her. It was shiny blue, with a pocket inside.

She opened it to a fresh page and wrote "Bess's Missing Locket."

Then she quickly looked around the park. Who could have stolen it?

Some third-grade girls were playing jump rope again, a few feet away. One of them looked over at Nancy. She laughed a mean laugh. It was Brenda Carlton.

11

Brenda wasn't very nice—at least she wasn't nice to Nancy. She always acted as if she thought she was smarter. And her clothes were prettier. And her handwriting was neater.

Maybe *she* stole the locket, Nancy thought. Nancy wrote down Brenda's name in her notebook. Then she wrote the other girls' names down, too. Laura Anderson, Rebecca Ramirez, and Katie Zaleski were there.

A minute later two boys zoomed up to Nancy on their bikes. They rode around the big tree in circles. Finally one of them leaned down and grabbed a backpack.

Is he stealing that backpack? Nancy wondered.

Nancy wanted to write down the two boys' names, but she didn't know them. Then she looked around again.

There were so many kids in the park!

I've got to hurry, Nancy thought. She wanted to get all their names—before the suspects got away.

She counted the names on her list. Eleven in all.

Too many suspects! Nancy thought.

And it was getting late. It was time for Nancy to go home. She put her notebook away and picked up her backpack from under the big tree.

But just as she was about to leave, a fourth grader, Karen Koombs, came up beside her.

While Nancy was watching, Karen picked up a jean jacket and started looking through the pockets. Then she put the jacket down and picked up another.

Nancy couldn't believe it. Karen was going through the pockets of the second jacket, too!

"What are you doing?" Nancy asked.

"Nothing!" Karen said. But she jumped when Nancy asked her. "Just looking for some gum. Why?"

"But those aren't your jackets," Nancy said. "It's not your gum."

Karen scowled. She looked angry. "What are *you* doing?" she said. "Spying on me?"

"No," Nancy said. "I'm trying to find out—"

13

"Did you ever think this might be my friend Melissa's jacket?" Karen asked. "She said I could have some of her gum. But I didn't know which jacket was hers. I looked in the wrong one."

"Oh," Nancy said.

Karen didn't say anything else. She just took the gum and ran off.

She's probably telling the truth, Nancy thought. But why was she acting so guilty?

Nancy hurried through the park and toward her house.

"Hannah! I'm home!" Nancy called when she reached the kitchen door. Then she raced up the stairs to her room.

"Hannah?" Nancy called again.

Hannah Gruen was the Drew family's housekeeper. She had been living with Nancy and her father for five years, ever since Nancy's mother died.

"In here," Hannah answered, but her voice was muffled. She was in the closet in Nancy's bedroom, cleaning it out. When she stepped out of the closet,

Nancy saw she had a piece of fuzz stuck in her gray-and-brown hair.

"What's wrong?" Hannah asked, seeing the unhappy look on Nancy's face.

"George and Bess are fighting," Nancy said. "They're never going to speak to each other again."

Hannah smiled a little and brushed the fuzz out of her hair. She sat down on Nancy's bed. Nancy sat down, too. She told Hannah everything that had happened.

"What should I do?" Nancy asked. "George and Bess are supposed to go to the movies with Daddy and me tonight. But they're so mad at each other, I know they won't go."

"Just let them cool down awhile," Hannah said. "They'll get over it. Maybe your father can take you to the movies on Sunday instead."

Maybe Hannah was right, Nancy thought. Bess and George might make up—sometime. But when?

Probably not by Sunday. Not in time for the movies, for sure!

3

Telephone Tricks

The next morning Nancy called Bess first thing. But Bess wouldn't even come to the phone—not until she found out who it was. She didn't want to talk to George.

"I'm coming over," Nancy said.

"Alone?" Bess asked.

"Yes, alone," Nancy said. She shook her head. "Can't you make up with George?"

"No," Bess said. "She lost my locket, and she doesn't even care."

"Well, I need both of you to help me solve this mystery," Nancy said.

"No, you don't. We can do it without

17

George," Bess said. "We'll solve it ourselves."

Nancy sighed as she hung up. Then she put on one of her favorite Saturday morning outfits—blue jeans, a pink sweater, and pink sneakers. She grabbed her special blue notebook and told Hannah where she was going. Then she walked to Bess's house. She was allowed to go by herself because it was only a few blocks away.

When Nancy got there, Bess was still in her nightgown. She had big fuzzy animal slippers on her feet.

"Let's sit on my bed and talk," Bess said.

Nancy liked Bess's room. Because it was upstairs, it had a slanted ceiling. When they sat on Bess's bed, the ceiling was low near their heads. It made Nancy feel cozy.

Nancy took out her notebook and showed the list of suspects to Bess.

"All these people were in the park," Nancy said. "So that means that they're all suspects."

"No, they're not," Bess said. "They

weren't all near the backpacks while I was jumping rope. Some of them were jumping rope with me."

She pointed to a bunch of names, and Nancy crossed them off.

"And some of them were playing on the swings when the locket was stolen," Bess said.

"Really?" Nancy said. "That's great." Bess pointed to more names, and Nancy crossed those off, too.

"Do you remember who *was* near the big tree?" Nancy asked.

"Of course," Bess said. "Karen Koombs was there. She was wearing a blue flowered skirt and a corduroy jacket. I saw her hanging around the backpacks by herself."

Nancy frowned. "She's one of my biggest suspects." Nancy told Bess what had happened when Karen was looking for the gum.

"She's my biggest suspect, too," Bess said, "because she steals things. Last year she stole some money from the office at school."

"Really?" Nancy's eyes grew big.

"Well, that's what everyone said, anyway," Bess said.

"Did they prove it?" Nancy asked.

"No."

"Well, then, maybe she's guilty and maybe she's not," Nancy said.

"Okay, but I still think she did it. Let's make a new list of the real suspects. The ones who were near the tree. Put Karen Koombs at the top," Bess said.

"Okay." Nancy wrote "New Suspects" in her notebook. Then she wrote "Karen Koombs." "Who else?" she asked.

"Jenny March was there," Bess said. "She was getting a gray sweater out of her backpack. I noticed because it didn't go with her outfit. She was wearing green tights with a blue-and-green jumper over them."

Nancy threw a pillow at Bess. "Forget what everyone was wearing!" Nancy said, laughing. "Just tell me who else was near the tree!"

"Mike Minelli was there. He was throwing something at a squirrel up in the tree. And a boy from fourth grade. I think his name is Ned Nickerson."

Nancy grabbed her pencil. Under Karen's name she wrote:

Jenny March
Mike Minelli
Ned Nickerson

Then she thought for a minute.

"Here's what I'm wondering," Nancy said. "Remember the yucky sandwich that the thief put in George's backpack? Where did it come from?"

"Maybe the thief had it left over in her lunch," Bess said.

"Or *his* lunch," Nancy said.

"Right."

"So I know what we have to do," Nancy said, jumping up. "We have to find out who eats peanut butter with mustard, ketchup, and relish for lunch."

"How are we going to do that?" Bess asked.

Nancy thought for a minute. "We're going to call up all the suspects and ask them."

The two girls raced downstairs. They huddled around the telephone in the family room. Bess's parents were outside working in the yard. The girls had the house to themselves.

Nancy looked up Karen Koombs's phone number in the school telephone book. Then she cleared her throat and dialed. Busy signal.

"Who's next?" Nancy asked. Jenny March's name was next. Nancy dialed the phone number. Mr. March answered the phone.

"Hello," Nancy said, trying to sound very serious and grown-up. "This is Nancy Drew. I go to Carl Sandburg Elementary School, and I'm doing a report. It's for a science project."

"No, no, no!" Bess whispered in the background. "Jenny's in our class. She knows there's no science project!"

"Uh, it's for extra credit," Nancy said, changing her story quickly.

Mr. March said, "Uh-huh," at the other end of the line. He sounded as if he wanted Nancy to get to the point.

"So anyway, can you tell me what Jenny usually eats for lunch?" Nancy asked.

Mr. March laughed. "Sorry," he said. "Her mother isn't here right now, and she makes Jenny's lunch. She and Jenny have gone shopping. Why don't you just ask Jenny yourself, at school?"

"Uh, right. Okay, I'll do that," Nancy said, hanging up fast.

"This isn't working," Bess said.

"Maybe not for the kids in our class," Nancy said. "But I think I'll try Karen one more time." Nancy dialed Karen Koombs's number. "Wish me luck!" she whispered.

Bess crossed her fingers.

"Hello, Mrs. Koombs?" Nancy said. "This is Nancy Drew. I'm doing a report for a class project at school. Can you tell me what Karen likes to eat for lunch?"

"For lunch? Oh, that's easy," Mrs. Koombs said. "My kids will eat anything—as long as it has peanut butter on it. So every day I just give them peanut butter with whatever I have in the house!"

4

Sniffing Out
the Proof

Karen must be the thief," Nancy said, hanging up the phone. She told Bess everything Mrs. Koombs had said.

"I knew it!" Bess said. "Let's go over to Karen's house and make her give me my locket back."

"We can't," Nancy said.

"Why not?"

"Because we don't have any proof," Nancy said.

"Whose side are you on, anyway?" Bess asked.

"Yours," Nancy said. "And I think Karen took your locket. But my dad says you have to have proof. And we

26

haven't *proved* that she stole your locket. All we know for sure is that she eats peanut butter for lunch."

Nancy picked up her notebook again. Bess peered over Nancy's shoulder as she wrote:

Question: Where did the yucky sandwich come from?
Answer: Karen Koombs's lunch!

"Okay, then let's go over to her house and *get* the proof," Bess said.

"How about this?" Nancy said. "We'll go to her house and climb a tree. Then we can look in her bedroom window. Maybe we'll see the locket. Or we can hide in the bushes until she comes out of the house. Then maybe we'll catch her wearing it."

"Climb a tree?" Bess said weakly.

Nancy laughed. "Sure. Why not?"

"You know I'm not good at climbing," Bess said. "And why do we have to hide in the bushes? Bushes are prickly."

27

"That's okay," Nancy said. "I can get someone else to help me."

Bess's face turned hot pink.

"You mean George. Okay, fine! Get George to help you!" Bess said in a grumpy voice.

"I will," Nancy said. "Because George is my friend, too. And if we can make Karen give the locket back, then you and George can be friends again. And we can all go to the movies."

"I'm not going to the movies with George, no matter what happens!" Bess announced. She stomped out of the room. Her animal slippers looked funny. The long doggie ears flopped as she walked.

Nancy picked up her notebook and quietly slipped out the back door.

What a mess, Nancy thought as she walked the two blocks to George's house. Now Bess is mad at me, too.

Nancy rang the bell at George's house. No one answered. So she walked around to the side. George was shooting baskets in the driveway with her dad. Nancy waited for them to finish. Then she told George about her plan.

"Okay," George said. "I'll help you get the locket back. I feel really bad that it's gone. But I'm not going to make up with Bess. Not until she says she's sorry."

"For tearing up your soccer picture?" Nancy asked.

George nodded. "And for calling me that horrible name." George didn't even want to say it again. But Nancy knew what she meant. Georgia. George hated her real name.

When Nancy and George got to Karen Koombs's house, they ducked into the yard. They hid behind some bushes. Then they circled the house and peeked in the windows.

"I can't see anything. We're not tall enough," Nancy said.

"I'll fix that," George said with a smile. She turned around and looked behind her. There was a small tree near the house in the backyard.

George climbed it easily. She sat on a branch facing an upstairs window.

"It's Karen's room," George called down to Nancy in a loud whisper.

Nancy looked around to be sure no one was coming. She didn't want to get caught spying into Karen's room.

"What do you see?" Nancy whispered back.

"I'll tell you when I come down," George whispered.

Nancy waited while George scrambled down the tree. When she got to the lowest branch, she jumped. George loved to jump from high places. She landed with a thump in the soft grass.

"Did you see the locket? Or anything?" Nancy asked.

George shook her head. "I couldn't see anything on her dresser. It was all piled up with clothes and papers and stuff."

"Hey—look," Nancy said. She pointed up to Karen's bedroom. Someone was peeking out at them from behind one of the curtains.

"Hi!" George called, waving.

"Why'd you do that?" Nancy asked.

"It's probably Karen. Maybe she'll come out," George said.

But an instant later the curtains snapped shut.

"Now what?" George asked.

Nancy shrugged. "Well, we could wait until two o'clock. That's when the ice cream truck usually comes. Maybe Karen will hear it and come out."

"It's October," George said. "The ice cream truck stopped coming at the end of summer."

"Oh, right," Nancy said. "Then we could ring the bell and pretend we're selling Girl Scout cookies. Or we could go home and make some popcorn and bring it over here. Maybe she'll smell it and come outside."

"Did you forget to have lunch today?" George asked.

Nancy looked at her watch. It was twelve-thirty. "Yes, I guess I did," she said, blushing. "Why?"

"Because you sound hungry," George said. "All your ideas are about food."

Nancy laughed. "I *am* hungry," she said. "Maybe we should go."

George and Nancy walked to the front yard. But as they passed the front door, Nancy sniffed the air. Something smelled good in Karen's house. Someone was baking cookies!

Suddenly the front door opened. A little boy came out. He had two cookies—one in each hand.

"Hi," he said with his mouth full.

"Hi," Nancy said, looking at the cookies. Her stomach growled.

"What's your name?" the little boy asked.

"Nancy. What's yours?"

"Jimmy," the little boy answered. He had a bowl-shaped haircut and pudgy knees.

"Mmmm," Nancy said. "Your cookies smell good. What kind are they?"

"Peanut butter," the little boy answered.

Peanut butter! Of course! Nancy thought. She should have recognized that smell. And peanut butter was Karen's favorite food!

"I'll bet your sister likes those cookies, doesn't she?" Nancy asked.

Jimmy nodded.

"Well, you know what I heard?" Nancy said. "I heard that your sister eats peanut butter every day. And someone told me that she even likes it with ketchup and mustard and relish. Is that true?"

"No, no, no," Jimmy said, shaking his head and laughing. "That's silly!"

"It is?" Nancy asked.

"Yes," Jimmy said. "My sister hates relish. It's her most unfavorite-est food in the whole world!"

5

Yuck for Lunch

Karen hates relish?" Nancy repeated the words, just to be sure.

Jimmy nodded his head. "I hate it, too," he said proudly.

Nancy gave Jimmy a pat on the head. Then she walked a few steps away. She felt confused.

If Karen hates relish, Nancy thought, then she wouldn't take a peanut butter and relish sandwich for lunch. So that meant Karen was not the thief.

Nancy's stomach growled again.

"I'm hungry," Nancy told George. "I think I'd better go home and eat lunch."

"Okay," George said. "I guess I'll go

home, too." George started to walk away. But then she called to Nancy.

"Hey, Nan! Why don't you have a peanut butter sandwich for lunch? With mustard and ketchup and relish!"

"Maybe I will," Nancy said with a laugh. "Maybe I just will."

When Nancy got home, she made a peanut butter sandwich—but with strawberry jam. Then she sat down at the kitchen table and took out her blue notebook. She opened it to the page marked "New Suspects." She crossed Karen Koombs's name off the list.

Now what? Nancy wondered as she took a big bite of her sandwich. She stared at the list some more. There were still three suspects left. Jenny March, Mike Minelli, and Ned Nickerson.

Nancy's mind was in a jumble. She poured herself a glass of milk and tried to think hard. Who had a good reason to steal the locket? she asked herself.

Then Nancy thought of a different question. Who was most likely to eat such a weird, yucky sandwich for lunch?

"I wonder what it tastes like," Nancy said out loud.

The peanut butter was still sitting on the counter. So was the bread. Nancy jumped up and went right to work. She spread peanut butter on a single piece of white bread. Then she added mustard. And ketchup. And—worst of all—relish.

"Here goes," Nancy said, holding her nose. She took a deep breath and then bravely took a bite.

"Blechhhh!" Nancy said. She almost spit the sandwich out right on the floor. But she knew better than that. So she ran to the sink. She spit it out there instead.

"What on earth are you doing?" Hannah asked, coming into the kitchen.

"I'm a detective," Nancy said after she had rinsed out her mouth. "I'm investigating."

"Well, what did you find out?" Hannah asked.

"I found out this sandwich tastes as bad as it looks!" Nancy said.

*   *   *

37

That night Nancy lay awake trying to figure things out. It was fun being a detective. She had already crossed one suspect off her list!

But it was not fun having Bess and George fighting with each other. Nancy needed a new plan.

The next morning when she woke up, Nancy called Bess on the phone.

"Are you still mad at me?" Nancy asked.

"No," Bess said. "I guess not."

"Good," Nancy said. "Meet me in the park by the big tree at two o'clock. I have some important news about your locket."

"What is it?" Bess asked.

Nancy lowered her voice and tried to sound mysterious. "I'll tell you when you get there," she said.

Then she called George and said exactly the same thing.

Then she ate breakfast with her father.

"Daddy," Nancy asked, "if Bess and George stop fighting, can we go to the movies this afternoon?"

"Sure," her father said. "Don't tell me they're still angry with each other."

"Yes," Nancy said. "But maybe I can fix that. I have a plan."

Nancy crossed her fingers for good luck. When it was almost two, she walked to the park.

When Nancy got there, George was waiting by the big tree. She had her hands on her hips.

"Why did you tell Bess to meet us here?" George asked.

Nancy looked around. Bess was not there.

"How do you know I called Bess?" Nancy asked.

"Because she came to the park exactly at two. But she left when she saw me," George said. "You tried to trick us, Nancy. And what's the big news about the locket?"

"There isn't any news," Nancy admitted. "I just wanted you and Bess to make up—so we could all go to the movies this afternoon."

"That's really dumb," George said.

Nancy blushed. "Well, when *are* you

and Bess going to make up?" Nancy asked.

"Never!" George said. "She tore up my soccer picture on purpose. I didn't lose her locket on purpose."

"I guess that's true," Nancy said. "But you're being just as stubborn as she is."

George frowned. "Hmmm. I'd *hate* to be as stubborn as Bess," she said. Then George and Nancy both laughed.

"Let's do something *fun*," Nancy said. "Like look for more clues. I still want to find out who stole Bess's locket."

"Aren't you ever going to stop being a detective?" George said.

"Nope!" Nancy said happily.

Nancy took out her notebook and looked at the suspect list. The same three people were left: Jenny March, Mike Minelli, and Ned Nickerson.

"I'll bet a boy did it," Nancy said.

"Why would a boy steal a locket?" George asked.

"Just to be mean," Nancy said. "That yucky sandwich was a mean trick, wasn't it?"

41

"Yes," George agreed. "But I still don't think a boy would steal a locket."

"Why not?" Nancy asked. "And a boy is more likely to have a yucky sandwich in his lunch, isn't he?"

"Maybe," George said. "But if you think a boy stole it, why don't you ask him?"

"Ask who?"

"Him," George said.

Nancy looked up and saw what George was pointing at. There was a boy riding his bike on the path in the distance.

And he looked exactly like one of Nancy's main suspects. It looked like Ned Nickerson!

6

Brenda's Sneaky Trick

Let's follow him," Nancy said, staring at Ned Nickerson. "Maybe we'll see him steal something else. Or maybe we can find out what he eats for lunch."

The two girls walked through the red and gold leaves toward Ned. But before they got very far, they heard a girl's voice behind them.

"Nancy! George! Wait!" someone called.

Nancy turned around and saw Brenda Carlton waving to them. Brenda was in Nancy's class at school.

"What does *she* want?" George said.

"I don't know," Nancy said, wrinkling her nose. "Let's ignore her."

43

"Nancy! Come back!" Brenda called even more loudly this time.

"Oh, well. Let's go see what she wants," Nancy said.

Nancy turned and walked toward Brenda. But she kept looking back at Ned. She didn't want him to get away.

"Guess what?" Brenda said when Nancy and George finally reached the swings. "I found Bess's locket."

"You did?" Nancy couldn't believe it. "Where?"

Brenda tried to keep a straight face. But a sneaky smile crept into the corners of her mouth.

"It's right here," she said. "Although I don't know why Bess made such a big fuss. It's not very pretty, if you ask me."

"Where is it?" Nancy asked again. She felt a lump in her throat. Nancy didn't want Brenda to solve the case. Not after all the detective work Nancy had done!

"It's right there," Brenda said, pointing at the ground.

44

Nancy bent down quickly and saw an old, rusty chain lying in the dirt. It wasn't a necklace chain. It was the kind of chain that usually hung from a ceiling light or a fan.

"That's not Bess's locket, and you know it," Nancy said angrily.

"It's not?" Brenda said. She opened her eyes wide and pretended to be surprised.

"No!" Nancy said.

"Gee," Brenda said with a mean smile. "I could have sworn it looked like something Bess would wear."

"Very funny," George said, glaring at Brenda.

Nancy didn't say anything else to Brenda. She just tugged on George's sleeve. Then the two of them turned around and walked away.

When they were far away, Nancy said, "Oooh! She makes me mad sometimes."

"Me, too," George said. "But forget it. I thought you wanted to spy on Ned."

45

"I do," Nancy said.

"Well, we'd better hurry," George said. "He's leaving the park."

Nancy and George ran to catch up with him. He was waiting at the corner to walk his bike across the street. Nancy called, "Hi!" as loud as she could.

"Hi," Ned said as Nancy and George came running up.

"Nice bike," George said.

"Thanks," Ned said. "It's new."

"Oh, cool! It has gears," George said. She stooped down to look at the wheels.

"Yeah," Ned said, grinning. "It's a ten-speed."

"Can I sit on it?" George asked.

Ned paused a minute. Then he said, "Okay."

He's pretty nice, for a boy, Nancy thought. Maybe it was because he was in the fourth grade.

Still, he was a major suspect in the case. Nancy couldn't cross him off the list. Yet.

"Uh, can I ask you something?" Nancy said when George had gotten off

his bike. "I'm doing a report about lunches. Do you take your lunch or buy it in the cafeteria?"

"Both," Ned said. "What a dumb question!"

Thanks a lot, Nancy thought. Maybe Ned wasn't so nice after all.

"Well, anyway," Nancy went on, "when you take your lunch, what do you usually take?"

"Cheese sandwiches," Ned said.

"Anything else?"

"Cookies," Ned said. "And fruit. And chips. And juice."

"I mean, do you ever take any other kind of sandwich?" Nancy said.

"Why do you want to know?" Ned said. "You're weird."

Nancy blushed. "It's for a report. I *told* you. For school," she said.

"Oh, yeah. You've got Ms. Spencer," Ned said. "She gives weird stuff for homework. I remember that."

"So can you answer my question?" Nancy asked. "What other kinds of sandwiches do you like?"

"Turkey," Ned said. "And tuna fish." Then he looked at his watch. "Gotta go," he said. He pushed off with his foot and rode across the street.

When he was gone, Nancy opened her notebook. She crossed Ned's name off the list. "I don't think he's the thief," she said to George.

"Why not?" George asked. "Just because he didn't mention peanut butter sandwiches? Or just because he's nice?"

"Just because," Nancy said. "It's a hunch."

"Okay," George agreed. "Now what?"

Nancy looked at her watch. The movie was starting in an hour. Oh, well, Nancy thought. Maybe she and her two best friends could go next week.

"Now we wait for school tomorrow," Nancy said. "Because that's when I'm going to solve the case."

"How are you going to do that?" George asked.

"Easy," Nancy said with a laugh. "There are only two suspects left!"

7

Bus Buddies

Hannah, make me an extra-big lunch, okay?" Nancy asked when she came downstairs on Monday morning.

"Poof!" Hannah said. She waved a wooden spoon as if it were a magic wand. "You're an extra-big lunch!"

Nancy laughed. "That's Daddy's joke," she said. "But really—Ms. Spencer told us to bring a big lunch today. Our class is going on a field trip."

"I remember," Hannah said. "To a pumpkin farm, right?"

"Right," Nancy said.

"Well, don't worry," Hannah said. "I've already packed your lunch, and I put a surprise in it for you."

50

"What is it?" Nancy asked.

"If I told you, it wouldn't be a surprise," Hannah said with a smile.

Nancy put her pink-and-purple lunch sack in her backpack and skipped out the door.

"Have fun!" Hannah called.

When Nancy got to school, all the third graders were lining up beside a big yellow school bus.

"Nancy!" two voices called. One was Bess's. She was lined up near the front of Ms. Spencer's class.

The other voice was George's. She was near the back of the line.

Nancy waved to George.

"Nancy! Over here!" Bess called again. She motioned for Nancy to come stand with her. "Sit with *me* on the bus, okay?"

"Okay," Nancy said. But she thought, I wish George could sit with us, too.

"Did you figure out who stole my locket yet?" Bess asked.

Nancy shook her head. Then she looked around. Mike Minelli was standing right behind her. She leaned close to Bess's ear and cupped her hands. "I've got it down to two suspects. Jenny and Mike."

Bess's eyes widened. She turned her head and looked at Mike sideways.

"He probably did it," Bess whispered to Nancy. "Jenny's too nice."

Nancy thought Jenny was nice, too. But that didn't matter. She was trying to be a detective. And Nancy's father said a detective always had to stick to the facts.

"Guess what I found out?" Bess said.

"What?" Nancy asked.

"I found out why Karen Koombs was acting so guilty."

"Really? Why?"

"Well," Bess said, "my mother talked to Karen's mother. And she says that Karen *didn't* steal any money from the office last year. But everyone thinks she did. So she gets blamed for everything."

"Oh," Nancy said. That made her feel bad. She was sorry she had put Karen at the top of her list.

A moment later it was time for Nancy's class to get on the bus. Ms. Spencer stood by the bus door with a big empty shopping bag.

"Put your lunch sacks in here," she said.

Nancy dropped her lunch sack in and followed Bess up the bus steps. Bess took a seat by the window. Nancy sat beside her in the middle seat. That left one space near the aisle in the big bench seat.

A girl from Nancy's class started to sit in it.

"That seat's taken," Nancy said.

"Oh," the girl said.

A minute later a boy tried to sit there.

Nancy put her hand on the seat. "This seat is saved," she said.

"I know what you're trying to do," Bess said. "You're trying to save a seat for George. But it won't work. Even if she sits with us, I won't talk to her."

"I wish you and George would make

54

up," Nancy said. "I'm tired of this fight."

More third graders piled onto the bus. They pushed and shouted, calling to their friends and trying to get the best seats.

Finally George arrived. She was the last person on. She tried not to look at Bess. But there were no other empty seats. So George had to sit with Bess and Nancy.

"Hi!" Nancy said cheerfully.

"Hi," George said in a low voice so that Bess wouldn't be included. She folded her arms across her chest and stared out the window on the other side.

Oh, boy, Nancy thought. This is going to be a long trip!

At last they got to the pumpkin farm. Ms. Spencer divided the class into small groups. Each group was given a measuring tape and a sheet of paper. They had to find the biggest pumpkin on the farm and measure it.

Nancy, Bess, and George were in a

group together. Nancy wrote the measurements down in inches. George wrote them down in metric. Bess did the measuring.

Then they had to weigh three pumpkins. There was a big, flat scale by the barn. The pumpkins were heavy, so grown-ups had to help.

By the time they were done, everyone was hungry for lunch.

Ms. Spencer stood by the picnic tables with the big shopping bag. "Your lunch sacks are here," she called out.

Nancy, Bess, and George found their lunches in the big bag. But Bess refused to pick a table and sit down.

"I'm not eating with George," Bess said firmly.

"And I'm not eating with her," George said.

"Fine," Nancy said angrily. "And guess what? I'm not eating with either of you!"

"What?"

George sounded totally surprised. Bess just stared with her mouth open.

"I'm sick of your fighting," Nancy said. "You were both wrong. George was wrong to put the locket in her backpack. But she didn't lose it on purpose," Nancy said to Bess. "And, Bess—you were wrong to tear up the newspaper clipping. You knew how special that was to George."

"But she was acting like she didn't care!" Bess whined.

"It doesn't matter," Nancy said. "You were still wrong. And now you're both acting like, well, like jerks!"

"Ooh! How can you say that?" Bess said, stamping her foot.

"Because friends are more important than lockets. Or newspaper clippings. Or anything else," Nancy said. "And you're acting like you don't know that."

Bess was quiet then, but her face said a lot. It said that she knew Nancy was right. George was blushing, too. Nancy had never seen George blush.

"So go ahead and eat your lunch— wherever you want," Nancy said in a

57

calmer tone of voice. "I'll be back in a minute. First I want to see what Jenny and Mike are eating."

Nancy turned her back on her friends and walked away. But when they weren't looking, she smiled. Maybe they would stop fighting now. At least it was worth a try!

It took only a minute for Nancy to find Jenny March and sneak a look at her lunch. Jenny was eating hot soup from a thermos. No peanut butter with relish was in sight.

Then Nancy wandered past Mike's table. She had to pass it three times. Finally she got the answer. Mike wasn't eating peanut butter, either. Just a ham sandwich and a huge bag of nacho chips.

By the time Nancy got back to her own table, Bess and George were smiling.

"We made up," Bess announced, as if it had been her idea.

"Really?" Nancy said. "That's great!" She hugged Bess and George both.

This was the best news she'd had all day!

"You were right," Bess went on. "Friends *are* more important than lockets."

George smiled. "And more important than newspaper clippings," she said.

"So anyway, did you find out who stole the locket?" Bess asked eagerly.

Nancy shook her head. She sat down on the picnic bench. "I guess maybe I'll never find out," she said glumly. "This mystery was just too hard."

"Oh, well," Bess said. She tried not to sound too disappointed.

But Nancy was the most disappointed of all. It was no fun being a detective if she couldn't solve the case!

Nancy opened her pink-and-purple lunch sack. She took out all the food.

"Hard-boiled eggs?" Nancy said. "I hate hard-boiled eggs! I can't believe this is the surprise Hannah packed in my lunch."

Just then Nancy heard Molly Angelo talking. She was a small, bouncy girl

59

with long curly dark hair and a good sense of humor. But she was complaining at the table behind them.

"Tuna fish?" Molly was saying. "I'm allergic to tuna fish! Why would my mother put that in my lunch?"

Nancy jumped up and looked at Molly's lunch. There were two tuna fish sandwiches, an apple, a box of juice—and a big piece of pumpkin pie. It was just the kind of lunch that Hannah always packed. Except that on normal days, Hannah put in only one sandwich and no pie. The pumpkin pie must have been the surprise—since they were going to a pumpkin farm.

Then Nancy saw Molly's lunch sack. It was pink and purple—exactly like Nancy's.

"You've got my lunch by mistake," Nancy said to Molly.

"Really?" Molly said. Nancy nodded. "That's good," Molly said. "Because if I eat tuna fish, I'll barf."

Nancy laughed and traded lunches with Molly.

Finally Nancy sat down with Bess and George again. But she didn't eat her food. She just sat there, staring off into space.

"What's wrong now?" George asked.

"Nothing," Nancy said, still staring. "It's just that . . ." Nancy's voice trailed off.

"What?" Bess and George both asked.

"It's just that I think I know where your locket is!"

8

Locket Found

You do? You know where my locket is?" Bess said.

"Just let me think a minute more," Nancy said, closing her eyes.

Yes! It all made sense, Nancy decided. A minute ago she had taken the wrong lunch by mistake because her lunch sack looked just like Molly's.

So maybe—just maybe—the same thing had happened on Friday. Maybe someone had taken George's backpack by mistake. Someone who had a backpack just like hers.

If Nancy was right, then Bess's locket wasn't stolen. It might still be in George's backpack.

Bess and George squirmed while Nancy was thinking. Finally she opened her eyes.

"Okay. I'm pretty sure I'm right," she said.

"Where is it?" Bess asked.

"In George's backpack," Nancy said.

Bess threw up her hands. "But we looked there! It was gone."

"No," Nancy said. "That's the problem. I don't think we looked in George's backpack. I think we looked in someone else's."

Quickly Nancy explained her idea. But George shook her head.

"That can't be right," George said. "I know it's my backpack because my notebook was in there."

"Are you sure? Maybe it wasn't *your* notebook," Nancy said.

George jumped up and ran to the school bus. Her backpack was inside, on the floor under her seat.

Nancy and Bess followed her.

As fast as she could, George unzipped the big zipper and pulled her notebook out. Then she opened it.

Inside the cover, in big red letters, was a name.

Ned Nickerson!

"I don't believe it!" George said. "You're right. It's not my backpack. It's his! And he has a notebook just like mine, too."

"Didn't you even look in your notebook on the weekend?" Bess asked.

"No," George said. "Why should I? We didn't have any homework." Then suddenly her face lit up. "I just remembered," she added. "The notebook came with the backpack. It was a free gift. That's why his notebook is the same as mine!"

Nancy smiled so hard her face hurt. It was the best feeling in the world— solving a mystery!

"You are the smartest person I've ever known," Bess said to Nancy.

"That goes double for me," George said.

The girls went back to the picnic table. But Nancy could hardly eat her lunch. She was too excited. She couldn't wait to get back to school and talk to Ned.

"Hey, does this mean Ned Nickerson eats gross peanut butter sandwiches?" George asked suddenly.

"I guess so," Nancy said. "But I can't believe it. Yuck."

When the bus got back to school, it was ten minutes after three. The school bell had already rung. Ned Nickerson was waiting outside.

"I think you've got my backpack," he said as George stepped off the bus.

"No, *you've* got *mine*," George corrected him. "You're the person who took the wrong one."

"Yeah. I guess I did," Ned said. "I should have noticed it, too. The straps were way too short."

"Well, here." George held out Ned's backpack and they traded. Then Ned checked to be sure his notebook was inside.

"I did all my math homework on Friday in school," Ned said. "But I got a zero for today, anyway—because I couldn't turn in my homework."

"Too bad," Bess said. "Maybe you can make it up."

"Yeah," Ned said. He started to walk away, but Nancy stopped him.

"I have a question," she said. "There was a really gross sandwich in there on Friday. Do you really eat peanut butter with all that stuff on it?"

"No way!" Ned said. "My uncle Matt did that."

"Did what?" Nancy asked.

"He made my lunch and put that sandwich in there—as a joke." Ned made a face.

"Your *uncle* plays jokes on you?" Nancy asked.

"He's nineteen years old," Ned explained. "And he's staying with us. He thought it was a riot. Ha-ha. It was so funny, I forgot to laugh."

"Yeah, and you forgot to throw it away, too," Bess said.

"I was saving it," Ned said. "I was going to put it on his plate for dinner on Friday night."

All of a sudden Bess started bouncing up and down. "George!" she said. "What are you waiting for? Open your backpack and see if my locket is still there!"

"Oh, sorry," George said. She unzipped the side compartment and looked inside. Bess's locket was curled in the bottom, right where George had put it. She took it out and handed it to Bess.

Bess closed her hands tightly around the locket and held it to her heart. "Thank you, Nancy—and George. You two are the best."

"It was nothing," Nancy said with a huge smile.

"Nancy did it all," George said. Then she was quiet for a minute. "You know, Bess, I really am sorry. I should have held on to your locket when you

asked me to. It was my fault that it got lost."

"That's okay," Bess said. "I'm sorry I tore up your newspaper clipping, too. But I have another one at home. I've been saving it for you."

"Thanks!" George said.

They gave each other a big hug.

"There's only one thing I want from both of you," Bess said.

"What?" Nancy and George asked.

"Pictures of each of you," Bess said. "I want to put your pictures in my locket. Nancy on one side and George on the other."

Nancy beamed at her two best friends. She was so happy. They were *all* friends again now, and that was all that mattered!

When she got home, Nancy took out her notebook. She opened it to the next blank page and wrote:

Today I solved another mystery— the Case of the Lost Locket. And I helped Bess get her locket back.

But the best thing about being a detective is that you can help people find things they lose—even if the thing they lose is a friend.

Case closed.

"If nobody did anything, nothing in the world would be different. Not everyone realizes that kids can make a difference too. Some adults think we can't, but we can."
— 9 year-old girl, talking about volunteering

 Help your community!

 Get in on the action!

Kids can make a big difference! Nickelodeon's The Big Help campaign gives you the opportunity to help in your community.

- **THE BIG HELP™ Book, by Alan Goodman:** Hundreds of ways—big and small—that you can help. Available wherever books are sold.

- **THE BIG HELP™ Telethon:** This fall, Nickelodeon will air a telethon that asks you and kids across the country to call in and pledge time, not money. Then you can spend the amount of time you pledged helping others.

- **THE BIG HELP™ Day:** A national celebration for kids, parents, and everyone else who participates in THE BIG HELP™

Why Nickelodeon? Nick believes that kids deserve to have their voices heard and their questions answered. Through events like 1992's Kids Pick the President, 1993's Kids World Council: Plan It for the Planet, and now the THE BIG HELP™, Nick strives to connect kids to each other and the world.

NICKELODEON

 A MINSTREL BOOK

Nickelodeon is a registered trademark of MTV networks, a division of Viacom International , Inc.

MEET THE NEWEST DETECTIVE ON THE BLOCK!

Meet Mr. Pin, a rock hopper penguin who can't stay out of trouble. With a taste for chocolate and a nose for clues, Mr. Pin and his sidekick Maggie tackle Chicago's toughest crime cases.

Mr. Pin: The Chocolate Files

The Mysterious Cases of Mr. Pin

and look for:

The Spy that Came From the North Pole: Mr. Pin Vol. III

coming mid-February 1995

by

MARY ELISE MONSELL

Available from Minstrel® Books
Published by Pocket Books

702-01

─CAROL ELLIS─

THERE'S A
TROLL
IN MY
CLOSET
I knew my closet was messy, but...Eeek!

THERE'S A
TROLL
IN MY
POPCORN
Tula's head-over-heals in trouble again!

THERE'S A
TROLL
IN MY
SLEEPING BAG
**What has pink hair, eight toes,
and lives in the woods?**

Available from Minstrel® Books
Published by Pocket Books

962-01

BRUCE COVILLE
Author of the <u>SPACE BRAT</u> series

WHO THROWS THE WORLD'S GREATEST TANTRUMS?
SPACE BRAT

IT'S TROUBLE TIMES TWO IN THE SWAMPS OF SPLAT!
SPACE BRAT 2:
BLORK'S EVIL TWIN

WHAT IS SQUAT'S EVIL PLAN?!
SPACE BRAT 3:
THE WRATH OF SQUAT

Available from Minstrel® Books
Published by Pocket Books

Simon & Schuster Mail Order Dept. BWB
200 Old Tappan Rd., Old Tappan, N.J. 07675
Please send me the books I have checked above. I am enclosing $_____(please add $0.75 to cover the postage and handling for each order). Please add appropriate sales tax). Send check or money order–no cash or C.O.D.'s please. Allow up to six weeks for delivery. For purchase over $10.00 you may use VISA: card number, expiration date and customer signature must be included.

Name _____

Address _____

City _____ State/Zip _____

VISA Card # _____ Exp.Date _____

Signature _____

835-05